This book belongs to:

....

....

Bright Sparks books have been created
with the help of experts in early childhood education.
They are designed to help young children achieve
success in their early learning years.

Retold by Sue Graves
Illustrated by Priscilla Lamont

Reading consultants: Betty Root and Monica Hughes

This is a Parragon Publishing book
First published 2006

Parragon Publishing
Queen Street House
4 Queen Street
Bath BA1 1HE, UK

ISBN 1-40547-968-X
Printed in China

The Gingerbread Man

p

Helping your child read

Bright Sparks readers are closely linked to recognized learning strategies. Their vocabulary has been carefully selected from word lists recommended by educational experts.

Read the story
Read the story
to your child
a few times.

Once there was a little old man an
a little old woman.
One day, the little old woman ma
a gingerbread man.
She made him very carefully.
Then she put him in the oven to b

8

Follow your finger
Run your finger under
the text as you read.
Soon your child will begin to
follow the words with you.

Look at the pictures

Talk about the pictures. They will help your child understand the story.

The little old woman made a gingerbread man.

9

Give it a try

Let your child try reading the large type on each right-hand page. It repeats a line from the story.

Join in

When your child is ready, encourage him or her to join in with the main story text. Shared reading is the first step to reading alone.

Once there was a little old man and
a little old woman.
One day, the little old woman made
a gingerbread man.
She made him very carefully.
Then she put him in the oven to bake.

The little old woman
made a gingerbread man.

Soon the gingerbread man was ready.
The little old woman opened the
oven door.
The little old man wanted to eat him.
But the gingerbread man jumped up.
Then the gingerbread man ran off.
"Come back!" said the little old man.

The gingerbread man ran off.

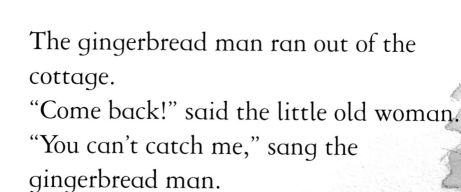

The gingerbread man ran out of the cottage.
"Come back!" said the little old woman.
"You can't catch me," sang the gingerbread man.

"Come back!" said
the little old woman.

The gingerbread man ran on and on.
The little old woman and
the little old man ran after him.
But they couldn't catch him.
"Run, run, as fast as you can!
You can't catch me,
I'm the gingerbread man!" he sang.

"You can't catch me!"

The gingerbread man ran on and on.
He ran past a cow.
The cow wanted to eat him.
"Come back!" said the cow.
"You can't catch me!" sang the
gingerbread man.

"Come back!" said the cow.

The gingerbread man ran on and on.
The little old woman, the little old
man, and the cow ran after him.
But they couldn't catch him.
"Run, run, as fast as you can!
You can't catch me,
I'm the gingerbread man!" he sang.

"You can't catch me!"

The gingerbread man ran on and on.
He ran past a horse.
The horse wanted to eat him.
"Come back!" said the horse.
"You can't catch me!" sang the
gingerbread man.

"Come back!" said the horse.

Just then, the gingerbread man came
to a river.
It was very deep.
"How can I cross the river?" said the
gingerbread man.

A fox saw the gingerbread man.
The fox wanted to eat him.

"How can I cross the river?"

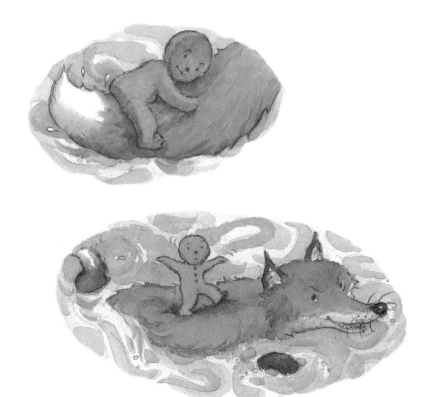

"I'll take you across," said the fox.
"Hold on to my tail."
The gingerbread man held on to the
fox's tail.
"I'm getting wet!" said the
gingerbread man.
"Hold on to my ears," said the fox.

"Hold on to my ears,"
said the fox.

The water was deep.
"I'm getting wet!" said the
gingerbread man.
"Hold on to my nose," said the fox.
The fox tossed the gingerbread man
into the air.
The fox opened his mouth.
Then, with a gulp, the fox ate the
gingerbread man.
And that was the end of the
gingerbread man.

The fox ate the
gingerbread man.

Look back in your book.

Can you read these words?

old woman

old man

gingerbread man

cow

horse

fox

Can you answer these questions?

Who made the
gingerbread man?

What did the
gingerbread man say?

Who ate the gingerbread man?

The End